The Bulletproof George Washington

An Account of God's Providential Care

by

David Barton

WallBuilder Press
PO Box 397
Aledo, TX 76008
817-441-6044

Nehemiah 2:17: "You see the distress that we are in...come, let us rebuild the walls that we may no longer be a reproach."

WallBuilder Press
P.O. Box 397
Aledo, Texas 76008
817-441-6044

Cover: The Union League of Philadelphia Art Collection.

Printed in the United States of America
ISBN 0-925279-14-5

Contents

Introduction and Foreword

George Washington, the Father of our Country, is well known to Americans for the accomplishments of his adult life: commander-in-chief during the American Revolution, statesman, and President. Few, however, are familiar with his youth or know anything more about it than perhaps the folklore surrounding the hatchet and cherry tree incident. Yet, possibly his younger years form the most important time for our national hero, for often it is what occurs in one's youth that determines what one becomes as an adult. Or, in the words of a contemporary proverb, "As the sapling is bent, so goes the tree."

It is for this reason that the account of not only what happened to, but of what happened around the young George Washington during the battle on the Monongahela is so important. Washington was only a 23 year-old colonel at the time of the battle and certainly the details of this dramatic event helped to shape his character and even confirmed God's call on this young man. Washington's part in the battle of the Monongahela is undisputably one of the most significant events of his early life--his life literally hung in the balance for over two hours. Fifteen years after the battle, the chieftain of the Indians Washington had fought sought him out and gave this account to Washington of what had happened during the battle:

> I am a chief and ruler over my tribes. My influence extends to the waters of the great lakes and to the far blue mountains. I have traveled a long and weary path that I might see the young warrior of the great battle. It was on the day when the white man's blood mixed with the streams of our forest that I first beheld this chief [Washington]...I called to my young men and said... Quick, let your aim be certain, and he dies. Our rifles were leveled, rifles which, but for you, knew not how to miss--'twas all in vain, a power mightier far than we, shielded you...I am come to pay homage to the man who is the particular favorite of Heaven, and who can never die in battle.

Today, few have ever heard about this important story. However, it has not always been the obscure account that it has now become, as suggested by the fact that I referenced more than three dozen older historical texts for this current work; and those texts were merely the ones in my own limited, personal collection.

The historical sources utilized for this work are diverse and range from personal records of the participants in the battle to details provided by Benjamin Franklin in his autobiography, as well as the research of prominent historians of earlier periods. I have included some excerpts from the original texts, some of which were published more than 160 years ago. When woven together, they not only provide an accurate and well-documented account of the battle, they also supply exciting and informative reading.

Additionally, several of the illustrations which appeared in those earlier works are included in this one. Other appendixes are provided at the conclusion of this work: a map of the battle area, a time line of the events leading up to and surrounding the tragic battle, and a listing of the primary and secondary sources utilized in this work.

It is my wish that through this account you will not only have a greater appreciation for the Father of our Country, but also a profound awe of the manner in which God sovereignly selected him and directly intervened in his behalf, preserving him for the important task of helping to bring forth, guide, and stabilize this great nation. The words spoken long ago by God to his beloved servant David seem to be descriptive also of the manner in which God used George Washington:

> I took you...to be a ruler over my people...I have been with you wherever you have gone...Now I will make your name like the names of the greatest men of the earth. (1 Chronicles 17:7-8, NIV)

May this account once again become widely celebrated throughout America!

David Barton

Chapter 1
The French & Indian War

In the seventy-five years from 1688 to 1763, England and France grappled in four European wars. In 1754, the fourth war erupted, known in American history as the French and Indian War. The final struggle between France and England for colonial supremacy in America was at hand.

This war marked the first time that the American colonies began to act together. From the first settlements, the individual colonies had been kept apart by prejudice, suspicion and mutual jealousy. But the original colonists were now dead; old antagonisms had passed away and a new generation had arisen. Yet it was not so much the growth of more tolerant sentiments as it was the sense of a common danger that at last led the colonists to make a united effort. The French and Indian War compelled the American colonies to join in a common cause against a common foe. For the first time, the separate histories of the colonies became lost in the more general history of the nation.

Although the contest began in 1754, the primary cause of the war had already existed for several years; it centered on long-standing territorial conflicts between the two nations. For ambitious men, and nations, acquiring large portions of the American continent was extremely desirable. Here was a country extending thousands of miles, covered by vast forests able to supply abundant timber to meet the demands of a growing world, containing boundless stores of mineral wealth, and with a climate varied enough to support diverse types of production. It was not surprising that the two nations were eager to obtain as large a share of these benefits as possible.

England had colonized the sea coast and had few inland settlements. Even though the English towns spread along the coast from Maine to Florida, the claims of England reached far inland. The English kings proceeded upon the theory that the voyage of Sebastian Cabot had given them a lawful right to America from the Atlantic to the Pacific. Their territorial claims were not limited to what they actually occupied.

The territorial claims of the French clashed directly with those of England. The French, who also had been among the earliest explorers and settlers of the continent, felt that they too had a special claim to a generous share of the New World. Unlike England, France had colonized the interior of the continent. Cities like Montreal and Detroit, early French settlements, were more than five hundred miles from the sea. Had the French colonies been limited to the north along the St. Lawrence River and its tributaries, there would have been little danger of territorial conflicts.

The French settlements were widely separated, stretching from Canada in the north to Louisiana in the south. The Governor of Canada proposed connecting these widely separated colonies by a chain of forts extending along the Ohio and Mississippi Rivers--in some places occupying lands already claimed by the English. The French began to push their way westward and southward, first along the shores of the Great Lakes, then to the Illinois River, on to the Mississippi River, then finally to the Gulf of Mexico.

The purpose of the French was to divide the American continent. They were drawing a great semi-circle around the English settlements along the eastern seaboard. If they could keep the English east of the Alleghenies, they could possess the larger portion of the continent for France. To accomplish this goal became the driving ambition of the French; to prevent it, the stubborn purpose of the English.

For years, the English fur traders of Virginia and Pennsylvania had frequented the Indian towns on the upper tributaries of the Ohio. Now the French traders of Canada began to visit the same villages and to compete with the English in the purchase of furs. Since the English colony of Virginia already claimed the territory lying between her western borders and the southern shores of Lake Erie, the French fur traders in the Ohio territory were regarded as intruders not to be tolerated.

To prevent further French encroachment, several prominent Virginians established The Ohio Company, whose purpose was to occupy the disputed territory. Robert Dinwiddie (the

Governor of Virginia), Lawrence and Augustus Washington (George's elder step-brothers from his father's first marriage), and Thomas Lee (president of the Virginia council) were its principal members. The Ohio Company constructed several trading posts between the Atlantic coast and the Ohio River. The Indians became accustomed to bringing their furs to these points to exchange them for English trinkets and goods.

The French were equally enterprising. Before the Ohio Company could dispatch a group of settlers to take possession, the Governor of Canada dispatched three hundred men to explore and occupy the Ohio valley. The French began to take possession: signs were nailed on trees, and plates of lead bearing French inscriptions were buried at numerous locations along both banks of the Ohio warning all who saw them that the country belonged to France. The French also wrote a letter to Governor Hamilton of Pennsylvania, warning him to encroach no further into the territory of the king of France. A line of French forts soon appeared on the Allegheny River.

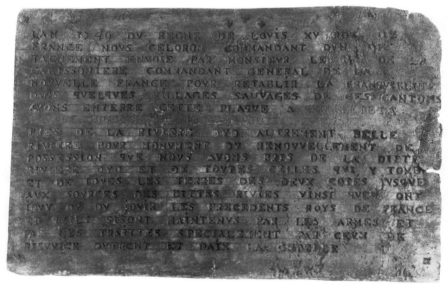

ONE OF THE LEAD PLATES BURIED BY THE FRENCH ON THE BANKS OF THE OHIO RIVER

When the Canadian governor began constructing his chain of forts, the English trading posts were viewed as obstructions to the French plans. Since those trading posts were symbols of English jurisdiction and were well known to the Indians, they had to be destroyed or converted to the use of the French. Accordingly, the trading posts were attacked by the French, were pillaged, and the English traders were made prisoners. However, the English would not permit themselves to be outdone in hostile activity. They responded in kind, regularly raiding Acadian farmers and French fishermen off the coast of Newfoundland.

The attempts by both nations to possess the disputed territory continued to escalate. The French continued to select and fortify new positions along the Allegheny, Ohio and Mississippi Rivers between their northern colony of Quebec and their southern settlement of New Orleans. The English, in the summer of 1753, opened a road through the mountains into the Ohio Valley and planted an English settlement. It was impossible that open conflict between the two nations could much longer be averted.

Chapter 2

George Washington
and the Great Meadows

Before proceeding to war, Governor Dinwiddie decided to file a final diplomatic objection with the French. A formal document was drawn up setting forth the nature and extent of the English claim to the Ohio Valley, sternly warning the French against further intrusion into that region.

NATIONAL PORTRAIT GALLERY, LONDON

It was necessary that this official remonstrance be carried to the French commander of its western forces, General St. Pierre, stationed at Erie. Who should bear this important parchment to its destination over 500 miles away? It was perhaps the most serious mission yet undertaken in America. A young surveyor named George Washington was selected to make the perilous trek. The governor summoned him from his home on the Potomac and commis-

PORTRAIT OF GOVERNOR DINWIDDIE

sioned him as ambassador. Washington carried the message from the seat of government in Williamsburg through the untrodden wilderness to Presque Isle on the shore of Lake Erie.

The twenty-one year old Washington departed on October 31st, 1753, to traverse more than five hundred miles through the pathless, wintry wilderness. Having procured an interpreter and guide, his tiny party plunged into the recesses of the wilderness, leaving every vestige of civilization. They endured snow and storms, crossed over mountain passes, and traveled through dense forests and into flooded valleys where they were forced to cross swollen, raging rivers on frail, dangerous rafts.

Arriving at the Youghiogeny River, they followed it to the Monongahela and then followed that to its junction with the Allegheny. That junction of the Allegheny and Monongahela Rivers was called "The Fork." It later became the site of the French Fort Duquesne (pronounced Dew-Cane), and then the location of the English Fort Pitt, from which sprang the present city of Pittsburgh. At the time Washington and his party passed "The Fork" it was uninhabited, but he noticed it and later reported it as an excellent site for a fort.

From "The Fork," Washington continued down the river twenty miles to deliver friendly greetings from Dinwiddie to Tanacharison (also called the Half-King), who was the great chief of the Southern Hurons. His friendship was being sought by both the French and the English. The chief received him with kindness; after Washington had attended a friendly council with the Indians, Tanacharison and three of his men accompanied him north the remaining hundred miles to the French encampment.

Here, on December 12th, at Fort le Boeuf, he found the French general, St. Pierre. Washington was admitted with great politeness, but the French general refused to enter into any discussion on the rights of England. He was acting, he explained, under military instructions given by the governor of New France. He had been commanded to eject every Englishman from the Ohio valley and he meant to carry out his orders to the letter. France already claimed the Ohio territory by virtue of discovery, exploration, and occupation; her claim now would be made good by force of arms. A written response was composed to be returned to Governor Dinwiddie.

THE ART COLLECTION OF THE UNION LEAGUE OF PHILADELPHIA

THE FIRST MISSION OF WASHINGTON

The scene is the interior of Fort le Boeuf. Washington is about to return with the French Commander's reply to the English governor of Virginia. His companions are a frontiersman, a guide, and a Dutch soldier as interpreter.

Washington was dismissed, but not before he had noted the immense preparations being made by the French. A fleet of fifty birch-bark canoes and a hundred and seventy pine boats was ready to descend the river to the site of "The Fork." The French, it seemed, as well as Washington, had noted the importance of that spot and were determined to fortify it as soon as the ice in the river should break.

With the rest of his party having departed to hunt and trap, Washington returned alone in the dead of winter and arrived at Williamsburg on January 16th, only eleven weeks after his departure. The boldness, judiciousness, and persistence with which he had met and overcome dangers, and his ability to successfully execute his assignment profoundly impressed his countrymen. The written records of his expedition were published throughout the Colonies and in England and resulted in widespread public praise for Washington.

COURTESY OF THE JOHN CARTER BROWN LIBRARY AT BROWN UNIVERSITY

THE

JOURNAL
o

Major *George Washington*,

SENT BY THE

Hon. *ROBERT DINWIDDIE*, Esq;
His Majesty's Lieutenant-Governor, and
Commander in Chief of *VIRGINIA*,

TO THE

COMMANDANT
OF THE

FRENCH FORCES

ON

O H I O.

To WHICH ARE ADDED, THE

GOVERNOR's LETTER,
AND A TRANSLATION OF THE
FRENCH OFFICER's ANSWER.

WILLIAMSBURG:
Printed by W I L L I A M H U N T E R. 1754

WASHINGTON'S JOURNAL PUBLISHED BY GOVERNOR
DINWIDDIE AFTER WASHINGTON'S RETURN

Negotiations had failed; a formal remonstrance had been tried in vain; now the possession of the disputed territory was to be determined by the harsher methods of war. Troops were raised in Virginia, and Washington was made lieutenant colonel and entrusted with a command.

Meanwhile, the French now occupied "The Fork." They had felled trees, built barracks, and laid the foundations of their new fort, Fort Duquesne. Colonel Washington set out on May 1st, 1754, to recapture this site by force.

On May 24th, the American regiment reached a location named the Great Meadows, still some sixty miles from Fort

Duquesne. Here Washington was informed that a company of French was on the march to attack him and had been seen along the Youghiogheny River, only a few miles away. Washington immediately erected a small stockade to which he gave the appropriate name of Fort Necessity. After learning from the scouts of the Half-King that the approaching French company was only a scouting party, Washington determined to strike the first blow.

Two Indians had followed the trail of the French and discovered their hiding place in a rocky ravine. The Americans advanced cautiously, intending to surprise and capture the whole force, but the French were on the alert. Seeing the approaching soldiers, they flew to arms. The engagement was brief but decisive. The French leader Jumonville and ten of his party were killed; twenty-one were made prisoners.

Washington returned to the Great Meadows and Fort Necessity where he waited for reinforcements. He spent the time of waiting by cutting a road twenty miles across the rough country in the direction of Fort Duquesne. A month of precious time now had been lost in waiting and only one small company of volunteers from South Carolina arrived at the camp. During that time, the French at Fort Duquesne had been collecting in great numbers.

Washington's whole force scarcely numbered four hundred, but he now marched to dislodge the enemy from Fort Duquesne. After advancing thirteen miles, his scouts reported to him that the French general, De Villiers, was approaching with a large army of French and Indians. Washington felt it prudent to fall back to Fort Necessity.

The little fort stood in an open space midway between two tree-covered knolls. On the 3rd of July, Washington's forces had scarcely secured the fort when the regiment of De Villiers, numbering some 1,200 men, came in sight and surrounded the fort. The French stationed themselves on the tops of the knolls, about sixty yards from the fort, where they could fire down upon the Americans. Many of the Indians climbed into the tree-tops where they were concealed by the thick foliage. For nine hours during a rain storm, from ten in the morning until

DEATH OF JUMONVILLE.

dark, a continuous shower of musket balls was poured into the fort upon them.

Although thirty of Washington's men were killed, the Americans bravely resisted, returning the fire of the French with unabated vigor. At length, De Villiers proposed that the Americans surrender. Washington, seeing that it would be impossible to hold out much longer, accepted the honorable terms of capitulation which were offered him by the French general. On July 4th, Washington's army, allowed to keep its equipment and provisions, marched out of the little fort they had so courageously defended and returned to Virginia.

After his return from the Great Meadows, Colonel Washington had public thanks voted him by the House of Burgesses for the gallant stand he and his men had made in the face of overwhelming odds. The Ohio Valley now remained in the undisturbed possession of the French, who continued to ravage and plunder the trading posts and settlements along the inner frontiers of the Colonies.

COURTESY OF THE ROYAL ONTARIO MUSEUM, TORONTO, CANADA

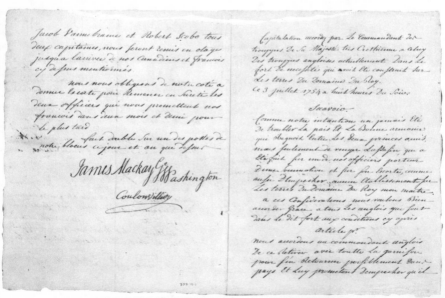

THE DOCUMENT OF SURRENDER WASHINGTON SIGNED AT FORT NECESSITY

Chapter 3
British Intervention

Individually, the Colonies were either too disjointed to take meaningful measures for their own common defense, or they were unwilling to take upon themselves the costly task of building forts and maintaining troops. Whatever the reason, the Colonies did not pose a unified threat to the French.

The British cabinet perceived that direct intervention from England against the French was eminent and that a war was inevitable. Without formally declaring war, the British ministry instructed the Colonies to cultivate the friendship of the Six Nations Indians and to renew their treaty with the Iroquois confederacy. Then, in order to stir up the Colonial authorities to some sort of mutual action against the French, the ministry advised that the Colonies form a union for their common protection and defense.

Accordingly, the Colonies unanimously resolved that "a union of the colonies was absolutely necessary for their preservation." Desiring that their common counsels, wealth, and strength might be directed against the French, a committee consisting of one representative from each Colony was appointed to draw up a plan of union. On June 14th, 1754, a congress was held at Albany, with delegates attending from Massachusetts, New Hampshire, Rhode Island, Connecticut, New York, Pennsylvania, and Maryland.

BENJAMIN FRANKLIN

About one hundred and fifty Indians of the Six Nations were present at the congress, with whom the convention made a treaty. The convention next addressed the question of uniting the Colonies in a common government. Dr. Benjamin Franklin, who attended the convention as the delegate from Pennsylvania, produced a plan subsequently titled "The Albany Plan of Union." In many ways his plan was similar to the later federal Constitution.

18

Under the plan, the new government would be jointly composed of representatives of the King and representatives from the Colonial assemblies. The new president and council would be vested with the power to declare war and peace; to conclude treaties with the Indian nations; to regulate trade with the Indians and to make purchases of uninhabited lands from them; to settle new colonies and make laws governing those colonies until they could become separate governments; and to

COURTESY OF THE HISTORICAL SOCIETY OF PENNSYLVANIA

JOIN, or DIE.

FRANKLIN DREW THIS FIGURE FOR THE PENNSYLVANIA GAZETTE TO ILLUSTRATE HIS ALBANY PLAN

raise troops, build forts, equip armed vessels, and adopt other measures for the general defense. To accomplish these things, power was given to impose any necessary duties or taxes in a means least burdensome to the people. Finally, all laws were to be sent to England for the King's approval.

Dr. Franklin provided his own account of the Albany meeting:

In 1754, war with France being again apprehended, a congress of commissioners from the different Colonies was...assembled at Albany, there to confer with the chiefs of the six nations concerning the means of defending both their country and ours...In our way thither [to Albany], I projected and drew up a plan for the union of all the Colonies under one government, so far as might be necessary for defence and other important general purposes...It then appeared that several of the commissioners had formed plans of the same kind...A committee was then appointed, one member from each colony, to consider the several plans and report. Mine happened to be preferred...and the plan was unanimously agreed to, and copies ordered to be transmitted to the Board of Trade and to the Assembles of several provinces.

Franklin's plan was signed by the attending delegates on the 4th of July, the same day Washington was retreating from Fort

Necessity and only twenty-two years before Franklin signed another document which he also assisted in forming--the Declaration of Independence. A copy of the Albany Plan was then distributed to each Colonial assembly and was sent to the King's council for approval.

The response to the Albany Plan from both the British government and the Colonial assemblies was the same--it was rejected. The British ministry disapproved of it because it gave too much power to the representatives of the Colonies; the Colonial assemblies rejected it because it gave too much power to the representative of the King. Perhaps this rejection by both sides is the strongest proof that it steered exactly in the middle, between the opposite interests of both America and Great Britain at that time.

Having rejected the plan of union, the British ministry proposed to the Colonial governors (most of whom were appointed by the crown) that they, with one or more of their council, should meet periodically to adopt measures for their general defense. They would be given power to draw on the British treasury for such sums of money as they needed, but those British funds were to be fully reimbursed by a tax to be imposed on the Colonies. The Colonies were not willing to agree to submit to taxation by Great Britain and rejected the plan. Franklin later commented on the rejection of his Albany Plan and on the events which followed:

> The Assemblies did not adopt it as they all thought there was too much prerogative in it; and in England it was judged to have too much of the democratic...I am still of opinion it would have been happy for both sides of the water if it had been adopted. The Colonies so united would have been sufficiently strong to have defended themselves; there would then have been no need of troops from England; of course the subsequent pretence for taxing America and the bloody contest it occasioned would have been avoided. But such mistakes are not new; history is full of the errors of states and princes.

As yet, there still had been no official declarations of war. Although the ministers of France and England kept assuring each other of peaceable intentions, Louis XV had sent out a powerful fleet carrying three thousand soldiers to reinforce the army in Canada. As their only alternative, the British determined to send an army to America to protect the frontier against the aggressions of France, being willing to accept any provincial troops that the Colonies might offer.

The British government, citing the establishment of the French forts on the Ohio and the attack upon Colonel Washington at Fort Necessity as justification for the commencement of hostilities, ordered General Edward Braddock to proceed to

BRADDOCK.

America with two regiments of English regulars to oust the French. Braddock, an Irish officer of forty years' experience, was now over sixty years of age. He was an officer who thought well of himself and was well thought of by others.

The night before Braddock sailed from England, he went with his two aides to see a Mrs. Bellamy and left her his will designating her husband as his beneficiary. He unfolded a map and remarked to her, displaying both his anger and melancholy, that he was "going forth to conquer whole worlds with a handful of men and to do so must cut his way through unknown woods." Braddock was the first British general to conduct a major campaign in a remote wilderness; he had neither precedents nor the experience of others to guide him.

Chapter 4
The Plans for War

On February 20th, 1755, the British soldiers arrived in America and dropped anchor in Hampton Roads, Virginia. The American colonists were greatly encouraged by the arrival of General Braddock with his two regiments, the first substantial force of British regulars ever to land on American soil. The colonists were now confident in the success of the campaign. It had seemed to them that all that was needed to drive the French home, or to whiten the fields with their bones, was the English army.

General Braddock proceeded to Williamsburg, the capital of the Colony, to meet with Governor Dinwiddie. Braddock requested that the Colonial governors assemble in Virginia for a planning meeting. Meanwhile, the strength of the two British regiments was being boosted by provincial enlistment. The British 44th regiment was commanded by Sir Peter Halkett, a superb officer, and the British 48th was commanded by Colonel Dunbar, an inept and cowardly officer.

The fleet next sailed up the Potomac to Alexandria, Virginia. There, on April 14th, Braddock met with the Colonial governors. The condition of Colonial affairs was discussed and it was resolved not to invade Canada, but to repel the French on the western and northern frontiers. Plans for four separate military campaigns against the French were approved. Lawrence, the British governor of Nova Scotia, was to secure that province according to the English version of boundaries. Johnson of New York was to recruit a force of volunteers and Mohawk Indians, with British pay, and capture the French post at Crown Point. Governor Shirley of Massachusetts was to equip a regiment and drive the French from their fortress at Niagara. Finally, Braddock, the commander-in-chief of all the campaigns, was to direct the most important campaign and would lead the British regulars and American volunteers against Fort Duquesne, driving the French from the Ohio Valley.

For the expedition against Nova Scotia, three thousand men under Generals Monckton and Winslow sailed from Boston on the 20th of May. On June 1st, they were reinforced by 300 more British troops and advanced against the principal French post in that region. After a bombardment of five days, the French set fire to their works and evacuated the country. With the loss of less than twenty men, the English were in possession of the whole of Nova Scotia.

The expedition against Crown Point on Lake Champlain, led by General Johnson of New York, did not secure its main objective, but did provide a victory for the soldiers in the campaign. In a major encounter near Whitehall, seven hundred of the French were killed with three hundred more wounded, while the Colonies lost scarcely two hundred.

The campaign against Niagara, with twenty-five hundred men under Governor Shirley of Massachusetts, was started too late in the year. The troops had proceeded to Osweego on Lake Ontario when the planned attack was abandoned. No more attempts were made against Niagara until after the formal declaration of war on June 9th of the following year.

George Washington was a participant in Braddock's expedition. Washington loved the military. Tradition holds that the first battles he commanded were the imaginary engagements in which the young Washington and his schoolmates played. In 1751, when Washington was nineteen, Governor Dinwiddie made him a major in the Virginia militia and gave him command of one of the four divisions into which Dinwiddie had divided the militia. Washington introduced a uniform discipline and infused his own military spirit throughout his command. He was promoted to colonel in 1754.

Shortly after, Governor Dinwiddie reorganized the militia, allowing no rank higher than captain. Because of these new military arrangements, Washington promptly offered his resignation and left the service in disgust. He retired to private life at Mount Vernon, determined to spend his life there in the pursuits of agriculture.

From the time of his arrival in America, Braddock had heard numerous highly favorable reports about Colonel Washington. In April 1755, Braddock invited him to Alexandria to join his military family as aide, retaining his previous rank. With this invitation, Washington's military ardor was again aroused. The thought that only a few miles away preparations were being made for an extensive campaign under the command of one of the most experienced generals of the British army stirred him and made him yearn to go back to the field. Washington was eager to study military tactics under a professional soldier of such high standing.

Washington's mother, concerned for his safety, hurried to Mount Vernon to persuade him not to accept the invitation, but was unable to discourage him. In their conversation, he reminded her: "The God to whom you commended me, madam, when I set out upon a more perilous errand, defended me from all harm, and I trust he will do so now. Do not you?"

BRADDOCK'S HEADQUARTERS IN VIRGINIA

After her departure, Washington left Mount Vernon for Alexandria. At Braddock's headquarters, the young colonel and the veteran general first met. Washington was welcomed into Braddock's military family with joy by Braddock's other two aides, Captains Orme and Morris.

Braddock's army was almost ready when a difficulty arose which nearly prevented the expedition. Even though American enthusiasm for Braddock's expedition was great, the public was reluctant to furnish the horses, teamsters and wagons which would be vital for the conveyance of military supplies and provisions during the expedition.

It was during this crisis that Benjamin Franklin came to the aid of the British army. Franklin, as Postmaster-General, had already been sent by the Colonial assembly to visit Braddock and attempt to dispel some of the violent prejudices Braddock held against the Americans. Franklin dined daily at the General's table. "The first capable and sensible man I have met in the country," Braddock wrote to his government concerning Franklin. Franklin described the dilemma facing Braddock:

We found the General at Frederick, waiting impatiently for the return of those he had sent thro' the back parts of Maryland and Virginia to collect waggons. When I was about to depart, the returns of waggons...amounted only to twenty-five, and not all of those were in serviceable condition. The General and all the officers were surprised, declared the expedition was then at an end... and exclaimed against the [British] ministers for ignorantly landing them in a country destitute of the means of conveying their stores, baggage, etc., not less than 150 waggons being necessary. I happened to say I thought it was a pity they had not been...in Pennsylvania, as in that country almost every farmer had his waggon. The General eagerly laid hold of my words and said, "Then you, sir, who are a man of interest there, can probably procure them for us; and I beg you will undertake it."

Franklin then turned with great effect to Pennsylvania, a colony of prosperous small farmers who were apathetic to the war but who possessed abundant resources. He advertised throughout local communities, explaining the generous terms of payment which the British offered the farmers for the lease of their wagons. The following excerpt is from Franklin's advertisement in Lancaster, Pennsylvania, on April 26, 1755:

Whereas, 150 waggons, with 4 horses to each waggon, and 1,500 saddle or pack horses are wanted for the service of His Majesty's forces...and His Excellency, General Braddock, having been pleased to empower me to contract for the hire of the same; I hereby give notice that I shall attend...Lancaster from this day to next Wednesday evening, and at York from next Thursday morning till Friday evening, where I shall be ready to agree for waggons and teams, or single horses...Note-- My son, William Franklin, is empowered to enter into like contracts with any person in Cumberland County.

B. Franklin

ADVERTISEMENT

Lancaster, May 6th. 1755.

NOTICE is hereby given to all who have contracted to send Waggons and Teams, or single Horses from *York* County to the Army at *Wills's* Creek, that *David M'Conaughy* and *Michal Schwoope* of the said County, Gentlemen, will attend on my Behalf at *York* Town on *Friday* next, and at *Philip Forney's* on *Saturday*, to value or appraise all such Waggons, Teams and Horses, as shall appear at those Places on the said Days for that Purpose; and such as do not then appear must be valued at *Wills's* Creek.

The Waggons that are valued at *York* and *Forney's*, are to set out immediately after the Valuation from thence for *Wills'* Creek, under the Conduct and Direction of Persons I shall appoint for that Purpose.

The Owner or Owners of each Waggon or Set of Horses, should bring with them to the Place of Valuation, and deliver to the Appraisers, a Paper containing a Description of their several Horses in Writing, with their several Marks natural and artificial; which Paper is to be annexed to the Contract.

Each Waggon should be furnished with a Cover, that the Goods laden therein may be kept from Damage by the Rain, and the Health of the Drivers preserved, who are to lodge in the Waggons. And each Cover should be marked with the Contractor's Name in large Characters.

Each Waggon, and every Horse Driver should also be furnished with a Hook or Sickle, fit to cut the long Grass that grows in the Country beyond the Mountains.

As all the Waggons are obliged to carry a Load of Oats, or Indian Corn, Persons who have such Grain to dispose of, are desired to be cautious how they hinder the King's Service, by demanding an extravagant Price on this Occasion.

B. FRANKLIN.

ONE OF FRANKLIN'S MANY ADVERTISEMENTS FOR BRADDOCK

Franklin told them quite candidly that it would be preferable for them to hire their wagons and teams to the British voluntarily rather than waiting until they were dragooned by the British army. He appealed not only to their patriotism, but to their pockets (or rather to their fears), as evidenced by the following notice:

To the Inhabitants of the Counties of Lancaster, York, and Cumberland

Friends and Countrymen,

I found the General and officers extremely exasperated on account of their not being supplied with horses and carriages, which had been expected...

It was proposed to send an armed force immediately... to seize as many of the best carriages and horses as should be wanted and compel as many persons into the service as would be necessary to drive and take care of them.

I apprehended that the progress of British soldiers... on such an occasion (especially considering the temper they are in and their resentment against us) would be attended with many and great inconveniences to [us], and therefore [I] more willingly took the trouble of trying first what might be done by fair and equitable means... you [now] have an opportunity of receiving and dividing among you a very considerable sum; for if...this expedition should continue (as it is more than probable it will) for 120 days, the hire of these waggons and horses will amount to upwards of £30,000, which will be paid you in silver and gold of the King's money...

If you are really, as I believe you are, good and loyal subjects to His Majesty, you may now do a most acceptable service and make it easy to yourselves... But if you do not this service to your King and country voluntarily when such good pay and reasonable terms are offered to you, your loyalty will be strongly suspected. The King's business must be done; so many brave troops, come so far for your defence, must not stand idle through your backwardness to do what may be reasonably expected from you; waggons and horses must be had, violent measures will probably be used...

I am obliged to send word to the General in fourteen days; and I suppose...a body of soldiers, will immediately enter the province for the purpose--which I shall be sorry to hear because I am very sincerely and truly your friend and well-wisher,

B. Franklin

According to Franklin, the needed results were achieved:

In two weeks the 150 waggons with 259 carrying horses were on their march for the camp. The advertisement promised payment according to the valuation in case any waggon or horse should be lost. The owners, however, alleging they did not know General Braddock, or what dependence might be had on his promise, insisted on my bond...which I accordingly gave them. The General, too, was highly satisfied with my conduct in procuring him the waggons...thanking me repeatedly and requesting my further assistance in sending provisions after him. I undertook this also and was busily employed in it.

Chapter 5

The Advance

In the latter part of April, the British general finally set out on his march from Alexandria to expel the French from Fort Duquesne (the site of the present city of Pittsburgh). A few provincial troops had joined the expedition and Braddock's army numbered nearly two thousand men, most of whom were British veterans who had seen service in the wars of Europe. He halted his march briefly at Will's Creek, where he constructed Fort Cumberland. On May 30th, he resumed the advance.

A select force was sent forward to open a road twelve feet wide in the direction of Fort Duquesne over the rugged, tree-encumbered ground. Several guides set out, followed by three hundred and fifty soldiers under Lieutenant Colonel Thomas Gage, accompanied by a working party of two hundred and fifty axmen. Following behind this group were the tool-wagons, two cannons, and the rear guard, all of which comprised the advance party. General Braddock followed this detachment with the main body, the artillery, and the provisions. The wagons and artillery moved along the road and the troops filed through the woods on both sides. The pack horses and the cattle, along with their drivers, made their way tediously through the trees and thickets. A body of regulars and the provincials brought up the rear.

ON THE MARCH.

The twelve-foot-wide road was opened with strenuous effort across mountains and rocky ridges, over ravines and rivers, and through the dense forest country between them and Fort Duquesne. Because of the wagons and heavy baggage, they were required to level the high spots and erect bridges over every creek.

The army, marching in a slender column, extended behind the work crew nearly four miles along the narrow and broken road. The baggage and supply wagons were so heavily loaded that the horses had great difficulty pulling the wagons over the rough, newly cut roads; this caused the entire army to make slow progress.

Consequently, Braddock became fearful that the French would entrench themselves in large numbers at Fort Duquesne. He considered it essential to move ahead rapidly and, if possible, surprise the French and cut them off. On June 19th, by the advice of Washington, Braddock left the heavy excess baggage behind with an escort of 600 men under the care of Colonel Dunbar. Then, placing himself at the head of 1,300 select troops with only those things that were absolutely necessary, Braddock proceeded by more rapid marches toward Fort Duquesne, leaving Dunbar and the remainder of the army to follow at their leisure. The army, now in two separate divisions, marched on.

Shortly after the army was split, Washington came down with a high fever that lasted for days and threatened his life. The physician was alarmed and Braddock ordered Washington to drop out of the march and remain behind until he recovered. With a wagon for his hospital, Washington remained under the physician's care for nearly two weeks. After two weeks, though still not fully recovered, he began to move forward very slowly and with great pain because of the constant jolting of the wagon over the rough roads.

As the army continued its march to Fort Duquesne, a body of Shawnee and Delaware Indians made an appearance. The Shawnees and the Delawares were in alliance with the British and had been faithful to them. They offered to side with the English in the coming conflict (they had frequently expressed a willingness to be sent by the English to harass and attack the French).

Washington, knowing they would be invaluable in a battle, strongly urged General Braddock to accept their offer. The General did so, but with such a cold indifference that he offended the Indian volunteers. That initial offense was so intensified by the subsequent neglect which they experienced from Braddock that they all departed. According to Franklin's account:

This General was, I think, a brave man, and might probably have made a figure as a good officer in some European war. But he had too much self-confidence, too high an opinion of the validity of regular troops, and too [low] a one of both Americans and Indians. George Croghan, our Indian interpreter, joined him on his march with one hundred of those people, who might have been of great use to his army as guides, scouts, etc., if he had treated them kindly; but [Braddock] slighted and neglected them, and they gradually left him.

Franklin.

Braddock, though not deficient in courage or in military skill, was totally unacquainted with the style of warfare necessary for the American woods. Braddock was self-willed, arrogant, proud and held the opinions of the Colonial officers in contempt. Thoroughly skilled in the tactics of European warfare, he believed that battles were to be fought in America just as in Europe--that soldiers could be marched directly against forest-fighters such as the French and the Indians as if they were going on a parade. Franklin had warned him about the Indian style of warfare.

In conversation with him one day, [Braddock] was giving me some account of his intended progress. "After taking Fort Duquesne," says he, "I am to proceed to

Niagara...for Duquesne can hardly detain me above three or four days..." Having before revolved in my mind the long line his army must make in their march by a very narrow road to be cut for them thro' the woods and bushes...I had conceived some doubts and some fears...But I ventured only to say, "...The only danger I apprehend of obstruction to your march is from the ambuscades of Indians...And the slender line, near four miles long, which your army must make, may expose it to be attacked by surprise in its flanks, and to be cut like a thread into several pieces..." He smiled at my ignorance and replied, "These savages may indeed be a formidable enemy to your raw American militia; but upon the King's regular and disciplined troops, sir, it is impossible they should make any impression." I was conscious of an impropriety in my disputing with a military man in matters of his profession and said no more.

Braddock could not bear to be advised by an inferior and when Washington repeated the same warning as Franklin and pointed out the danger of ambushes and the need for scouting parties, Braddock flew into a rage. He strode up and down in his tent and said that it was high times when a Colonial buckskin could teach a British general how to fight. "The Indians," said Braddock, "may frighten continental troops, but they can make no impression on the King's regulars!"

By July 7th, the column had arrived within twelve miles of Fort Duquesne and its difficulties seemed almost over. The British now felt that the French and their allies were not in great numbers or some type of confrontation would have already occurred, especially since the Indians greatly disliked artillery and battling from within the confines of a fort.

The following day, July 8th, the forward detachment had reached the junction of the Youghiogheny and Monongahela Rivers. That evening, the friendly Indians showed themselves a second time to offer their services. For the second time, Washington intervened on their behalf and explained to Braddock the Indian's style of warfare, of laying ambushes and of

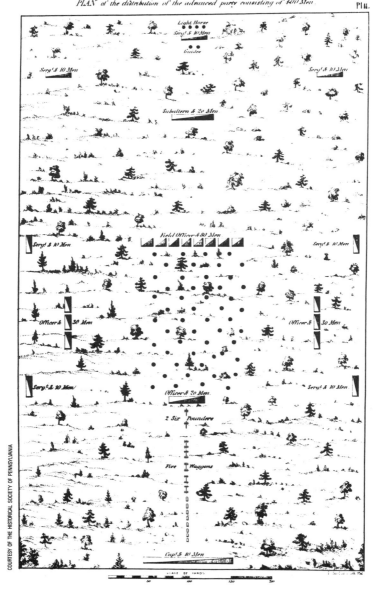

A MAP SHOWING THE ARRANGEMENT OF THE ADVANCE PARTY AND THE WORKERS

fighting from behind trees. As scouts, they could go ahead of the army and reconnoiter the woods and ravines to uncover any waiting ambush. Washington again urged Braddock to receive them, but Braddock, confident in the courage of his own troops, scorned their assistance and firmly refused their offer. He not only disdained Washington's advice, he again offended the Indians by his rudeness. His unfortunate decision sealed the fate of the following day.

Chapter 6

The Battle at the Monongahela

Early the next morning, July 9th, 1755, the army crossed the river and continued its march along the southern shore of the Monogahela. Still there was no sign of any enemy. At noon, from the heights above the Monongahela, Washington looked back upon the ascending army which had just crossed the stream for the second time, now only ten miles from Fort Duquesne. The companies, in their crimson uniforms, with shining weapons and floating banners, were marching gaily to cheerful music as they entered the forest.

Washington was often heard to say that the most beautiful spectacle he ever beheld was the display of British troops on this eventful morning:

> Every man was neatly dressed in full uniform; the soldiers were arranged in columns, and marched in exact order; the sun gleamed from their burnished arms; the river flowed tranquilly on their right, and the deep forest overshadowed them with solemn grandeur on their left. Officers and men were equally inspirited with cheering hopes and confident anticipations.

The army, its slender line nearly four miles long, moved forward with military precision and in fine spirits. Being only a few miles from Fort Duquesne, the troops felt confident that within a few hours they would be its master. To all appearance, the country was as uninhabited as on the morning of creation, but appearances were deceitful.

France was not willing to give up Fort Duquesne without a struggle. Even though the fort had been receiving reinforcements for two months, the French forces were still unevenly matched against Braddock's greater numbers. Even the Indian allies of the French realized the disparity between the sizes of the two armies. Having been kept abreast of Braddock's progress by the reports of their scouts, the French had determined that an ambush would be their most effective defense.

34

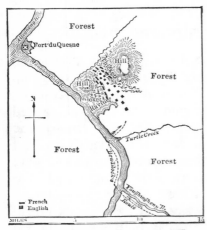

SCENE OF BRADDOCK'S DEFEAT, 1755.

The night before the battle, the French commander of Fort Duquesne, with great difficulty, persuaded the Indians to join in the ambush against the British. A force of 72 French regulars, 146 Canadian militiamen, and 637 Indians (a combined force of 855) set out from Duquesne to harass and annoy the English, not intending to face them in serious battle. The French, completely familiar with the territory, laid an ambush at a point seven miles from the fort. They were just reaching the spot and settling into their positions when the first British troops came into sight.

It was nearly one o'clock in the afternoon; Colonel Thomas Gage's forward detachment of three hundred and fifty soldiers and two hundred and fifty workers* and axmen was progressing up an incline. A few guides and some feeble flanking parties were in the advance. The General followed slightly behind the forward detachment with his columns of artillery, baggage, and the main body of the army. Although only a small distance intervened between these first two groups, Dunbar's division, with the heavy baggage, was now more than 40 miles to the rear. In this order the forward troops proceeded until they reached a spot with dense undergrowth and a hill on the right and a dry hollow on the left.

Gage's forward detachment had just crossed a shallow ravine when his scouts and flanking-parties came running back. At the same instant, Gordon, the engineer who was marking out the road, spotted an Indian running toward him. The Indian pulled up short and waved his hat over his head.

---

* Some early historical accounts indicate that Daniel Boone (1734-1820), a contemporary of George Washington, may have been a member of this work party.

A quick and heavy fire was immediately heard. The enemy now revealed its presence by the discharge of weapons. A shower of musketballs was poured into the front of Gage's company, doing extensive damage by sending metallic messengers of death among the unsuspecting soldiers. A storm of bullets, piercing the flesh and shattering the bones, swept the astounded ranks. To the British, it was like a supernatural attack from invisible spirits; not a musket was seen; the enemy was not visible. The blue smoke rising up after every discharge revealed that the firing came from the trees. The disconcerted soldiers fired into the woods at random, but without effect, doing little more than to sliver the bark from trees and to cut saplings.

The Indians were unerring marksmen. Crash followed crash in rapid succession. The ground was littered with the dead and the dying. The horses, many wounded by bullets and all in a frenzy, reared and plunged, and tore along the road, dragging wagons after them, trampling the living and the dead. The teamsters and axmen fled. There was no defence that could be made; the ranks were in utter confusion. Still a deadly storm of bullets fell upon them.

THE AMBUSH

The feeble return fire merely hit the rocks or was buried in the gigantic trees. The Indians were laughing derisively at the powerless struggles of their victims.

Gage's men panicked; the confusion became even greater. The men fired constantly, but could see no enemy. In the Court of Inquiry held by the British authorities after the battle, none of the English involved in the fight could say they had seen even a hundred of the enemy; and "many of the officers, who were in the heat of the action the whole time, would not assert that they saw one." Every volley from their hidden foe flew into the crowded ranks of the British with deadly certainty.

Braddock, hearing the intensity of the firing and knowing that his front detachment was seriously engaged, moved up rapidly with the main column, leaving Sir Peter Halkett with 400 men, including most of the Virginia provincials, to guard the baggage. Before Braddock could reinforce them, Gage's men had retreated, leaving their six-pounders (cannons capable of firing six-pound projectiles) in the hands of the enemy. The retreating men collided with the advancing men and artillery which were coming to their aid, mixing the two regiments together and throwing the entire army into confusion.

The soldiers were unable to determine whom they were fighting. Seeing their officers and comrades falling around them at every discharge from the woods, they became so panic-stricken that they were uncertain where to go or what to do. They remained stationary, huddled together in several frightened groups in the midst of the ravine, some facing one way and some another, firing their guns at random. All were exposed without shelter to the bullets that pelted them like hail. The intense, level-headed efforts of the officers to restore order were unsuccessful.

The hundred or so Virginia provincials, exhibiting greater savvy than the others, adopted the Indian style of warfare, fighting gallantly according to backwoods custom. Each man found a tree from behind which he fired whenever an arm, head, or any portion of an enemy became visible.

Braddock was furious about this skulking mode of battle--it was adverse to the rules of his profession, contrary to his ideas of courage and discipline. He issued a foolish yet stern order that none of the troops should protect themselves behind trees.

He then busied himself in efforts to form his men into regular platoons and columns, according to the rules of military tactics, even beating his men with his sword if they attempted to take cover behind trees or fallen logs. But while he was engaged in these futile endeavors, the French and Indians, in the concealment of ravines, and from behind rocks and trees, continued to single out their victims. The Indians, having a brightly colored target, virtually unknown in forest warfare, were playing deadly havoc: the beautiful red coats were targets they could not miss.

Although the typical British regular was brave in more conventional dangers, fighting a deadly enemy he could not see was something completely new. The scene was capable of intimidating the boldest of heart. The yells of the Indians, the panic of the soldiers, the frantic running of wounded horses, the unceasing rattle of musketry, the storm of leaden hail, the continual dropping of the dead, the groans of the wounded--all combined to form a scene of complete despair.

Braddock was a lion in combat. He continued undaunted while being showered with bullets, having five horses shot out from under him; however, his reckless courage was not turning the tide of the battle. His secretary was killed and both his English aides were wounded. Washington, the only uninjured aide of the general, rode over every part of the field carrying the general's orders.

Halkett's 400 men at the tail of the column were faring somewhat better than the main body, although Sir Peter Halkett himself was killed, and his son, while trying to help him, was shot dead by his side.

The events occurring around Colonel Washington during the battle provide a compelling proof not only of God's care, but of His direct intervention in behalf of Washington. Although Washington still had not completely recovered from his illness, he remained faithful to his duty, unflinching in the face of disaster. Carrying the general's orders to subordinates in all parts of the field made him a conspicuous mark to the enemy, who did not fail to take advantage of it. One who was watching Washington during the battle reported, "I expected every moment to see him fall. Nothing but the superintending care of Providence could have saved him."

Following the battle, the Indians testified that they had specifically singled him out and repeatedly shot at him, but without effect. They became convinced that he was protected by an Invisible Power and that no bullet could harm him. Two horses had been shot from under him; four times his coat had been torn by musket balls; but Washington escaped without injury. Shielded by God's hand, he was untouched by bullet or bayonet, arrow or tomahawk, even though scores of victims fell beside him.

It was a purely Indian-style fight, more one-sided than had ever occurred in the history of woodland warfare. The pandemonium had lasted over two hours. A hail of bullets that hardly tested the aim of the French and the Indians had been poured into the British army. It was butchery rather than a battle.

Finally, Braddock was shot in his right side and sank to the ground wounded. He, along with the rest of the officers on horseback, had been a special target. The Indians had singled them out, and every mounted officer, except Washington, was slain before Braddock fell. Upon Braddock's fall, the regular troops fled in confusion. It became a race for life by every man who could drag his legs behind him.

The battle had became a rout. Everything was abandoned to the enemy--wagons, guns, artillery, cattle, horses, baggage, provisions, and £25,000 in specie. Even the private papers of the general were left on the field.

The forest was strewn with the dead. The Indians emerged from their concealments with tomahawk and scalping-knife to seize their bloody trophy of scalps from the dead and from the wounded who were still struggling on the ground. Their tomahawks soon numbered the wounded with the slain.

Of three companies of Virginia troops, scarcely thirty men were left alive. Washington placed himself at the head of the thirty remaining Virginians, whom Braddock, in his contempt, had kept in the rear, and covered the panicked flight of the ruined army, enabling the shattered British remnant to retreat.

DEFEAT OF BRADDOCK.

The brutality of the battle was indicated by the number of casualties. Seven hundred and fourteen of the soldiers had been killed or wounded; and, of eighty-six officers, twenty-six were killed, and thirty-seven more were wounded. The losses of the French and Indians were slight, amounting to only three officers and thirty men killed, and as many others wounded.

Fortunately for the British, the Indians were so elated over their unexpected success and were so eager to secure the rich spoils of the British, that, instead of pursuing the retreating army and destroying it, they remained upon the field. They reveled on the battlefield--they had never known such a rich harvest of scalps and booty.

Washington showed great skill while directing the retreat of the remains of the army. Braddock, unable to mount a horse, was hurried from the field in a litter. About a mile from the scene, his wounds were dressed. The army continued to retreat rapidly until it joined the heavy baggage division under Dunbar, forty miles in the rear. For days Braddock lingered in great pain. By Franklin's report:

> Captain Orme, who was one of the General's aides-de-camp and, being grievously wounded, was brought off with [Braddock] and continued with him to his death, which happened in a few days, told me that [Braddock] was totally silent all the first day and at night only said, "Who would have thought it?"; that he was silent again the following day, only saying at last, "We shall better know how to deal with them another time," and died a few minutes after.

Braddock, who was being treated by Dr. James Craik, a close personal friend of Washington, died near the Great Meadows, a mile west of Fort Necessity. During the night, Washington read the funeral service of the Anglican church over his grave by torch-light. Braddock had been buried in the middle of the road and wagons were rolled over the fresh mound of dirt to keep his remains from being found and desecrated by any Indians which might pursue.

BURIAL OF BRADDOCK.

No attempt, however, was ever made at pursuit. With the army of Braddock annihilated, the French, conscious that the British army posed no imminent threat, left the starving, staggering, bleeding remains to struggle back to Virginia. The victors returned to Fort Duquesne (the Indian chiefs wearing the coats, boots, and decorations of the slain British officers) to rejoice over their unexpected victory and to prepare for another assault, should the British ever attempt to return.

An English officer, Colonel James Smith, captured before the battle on the Monongahela, was being held captive at Fort

Duquesne. His personal narrative provides a vivid portrayal of the scenes which transpired at the fort before, during, and after the battle. He reports that Indian scouts for the French were constantly watching the British army from mountain crags and from within the depths of the forest. Every day, runners returned to the fort with their report.

In the late afternoon of July 9th, the day of the battle, the triumphant shouts of fleet-footed runners were heard in the forest, bringing the initial news of the great victory. They reported that the English were huddled together in a narrow ravine from which escape was almost impossible and that they were in utter confusion. The concealed Indians were shooting down the British as fast as they could load and fire; before sundown all would be killed.

Later, a larger band of about a hundred Indians appeared, yelling and shrieking in frantic, boisterous joy. It was the greatest victory they had ever known, or even imagined. The Indians were shocked, even stunned, at both the quantity and the richness of their plunder. Braddock's army had been laden not only with all the conveniences, but with many luxuries as well--it was more than the Indians could carry away. They returned to the fort stooping beneath the load of caps, canteens, muskets, swords, bayonets, and rich uniforms which they had stripped from the dead. Most had dripping, bloody scalps, and several had money. Colonel Smith wrote :

> Those that were coming in and those that had arrived kept a constant firing of small-arms, and also of the great guns in the fort, which was accompanied by the most hideous shouts and yells from all quarters; so that it appeared to me as if the infernal regions had broken loose. About sundown I beheld a small party coming in with about a dozen prisoners, stripped naked, with their hands tied behind their backs. Their faces, and parts of their bodies were blackened. These prisoners they burned to death on the banks of the Allegheny river, opposite to the fort. I stood on the fort walls until I beheld them begin to burn one of these men.

They tied him to a stake and kept touching him with fire-brands, red-hot irons, etc., and he screaming in the most doleful manner. The Indians, in the meantime, were yelling like infernal spirits. As this scene was too shocking for me to behold, I returned to my lodgings, both sorry and sore. The morning after the battle, I saw Braddock's artillery brought into the fort. The same day also I saw several Indians in the dress of British officers, with the sashes, half moons, laced hats, etc., which the British wore.

THE INDIAN ALLIES OF THE FRENCH RETURNING HOME AFTER BRADDOCK'S DEFEAT DRESSED IN THE SPOIL OF THE BRITISH ARMY.

Chapter 7
The Return to Fort Cumberland

The scene at Dunbar's camp was one of total confusion. The terrorized retreating British regulars had arrived at the camp, and the panic they brought with them instantly gripped Dunbar and his troops.

Of the three British military leaders, Braddock and Sir Peter Halkett were now dead. The command of the army now fell upon the remaining leader, Dunbar. Dunbar was a man of incompetence and no courage. Although he now had about 1,000 men, he made no attempt to recover any of the lost provisions.

On July 12th, pretending to have the orders of the dying general, Dunbar ordered the remainder of the artillery, ammunition, heavy baggage, and provisions to be destroyed so that he would have additional horses to assist his hurried retreat to Fort Cumberland, one hundred and twenty miles away.

On July 17th, Washington and the disconsolate army reached Fort Cumberland. Several fugitives had already arrived and spread reports of the disaster throughout the countryside. Washington, knowing the terrible anxiety of his family, immediately wrote to his mother.

July 18, 1755.

Honored Madam:

As I doubt not but you have heard of our defeat, and perhaps had it represented in a worse light, if possible, than it deserves, I have taken this earliest opportunity to give you some account of the engagement as it happened, within ten miles of the French fort, on Wednesday the 9th...

We marched to that place, without any considerable loss, having only now and then a straggler picked up by the French and scouting Indians. When we came there, we were attacked by a party of French and Indians...our [force] consisted of about one thousand three hundred well-armed troops, chiefly regular soldiers, who were struck with such a panic that they behaved with more cowardice than it is possible to conceive. The officers behaved gallantly, in order to encourage their men, for which they suffered greatly, there being nearly sixty killed and wounded; a large proportion of the number we had.

The Virginia troops showed a good deal of bravery, and were nearly all killed; for I believe, out of three companies that were there, scarcely thirty men are left alive. Captain Peyrouny, and all his officers down to a corporal, were killed.

Captain Polson had nearly as hard a fate, for only one of his was left. In short, the dastardly behavior of those they call regulars exposed all others that were inclined to do their duty to almost certain death; and, at last, in despite of all the efforts of the officers to the contrary, they ran, as sheep pursued by dogs, and it was impossible to rally them.

The General was wounded, of which he died three days after. Sir Peter Halkett was killed in the field, where died many other brave officers. I luckily escaped without a wound, though I had four bullets through my coat, and two horses shot under me. Captains Orme and Morris, two of the aids-de-camp, were wounded early in the engagement, which rendered the duty harder upon me, as I was the only person then left to distribute the General's orders, which I was scarcely able to do, as I was not half recovered from a violent illness, that had confined me to my bed and a wagon for above ten days. I am still in a weak and feeble condition, which induces me to halt here two or three days in the hope of recovering a little strength, to enable me to proceed homewards; from whence, I fear, I shall not be able to stir till toward September...I am, honored Madam, your most dutiful son.

G. Washington

On the same day, he wrote his brother, John A. Washington:

> As I have heard, since my arrival at this place [Fort Cumberland], a circumstantial account of my death and dying speech, I take this early opportunity of contradicting the first, and of assuring you, that I have not as yet composed the latter. But, by the all-powerful dispensations of Providence, I have been protected beyond all human probability or expectation; for I had four bullets through my coat, and two horses shot under me, yet escaped unhurt, although death was leveling my companions on every side of me!

To Governor Dinwiddie, he wrote of what he called the "dastardly behavior" of the regulars, saying:

> They broke and ran as sheep before hounds, leaving the artillery, ammunition, provisions, baggage, and in short everything a prey to the enemy; and when we endeavored to rally them...it was with as little success as if we had attempted to stop the wild bears of the mountains, or the rivulets with our feet.

On his arrival at Fort Cumberland, Dunbar received requests from the Governors of Virginia, Maryland, and Pennsylvania to post British troops along the frontiers to offer some protection to the settlers. Although it was still midsummer, Dunbar felt he should enter winter quarters with his troops. He decided to evacuate Fort Cumberland and withdraw the regulars to Philadelphia for winter-quarters. Accordingly, the next day Dunbar and the British army retreated, leaving the whole frontier open to the pillage of the French and Indians. Regarding Dunbar's decision, Benjamin Franklin quipped:

> Dunbar continued his hasty march thro' all the country, not thinking himself safe till he arrived at Philadelphia, where the inhabitants could protect him. This whole transaction gave us Americans the first suspicion that our exalted ideas of the prowess of British regulars had not been well founded.

Franklin, for the wagons he had obtained, had issued personal bonds totalling a large amount. With these wagons and horses now lost, the owners pressed Franklin to make restitution of their property. Franklin would have paid the debt had he been able, but he was not, having already advanced considerable money for the campaign. The owners began to sue Franklin, which could have led to his ruin. Franklin described the tenuous situation and its resolution:

> As soon as the loss of the waggons and horses was generally known, all the owners came upon me for the valuation which I had given bond to pay. Their demands gave me a great deal of trouble. I acquainted them that the money was ready in the paymaster's hands, but that orders for paying it must first be obtained from General Shirley, and that I had applied for it...and they must have patience. All this was not sufficient to satisfy, and some began to sue me. General Shirley at length relieved me from this terrible situation by appointing commissioners to examine the claims and ordering payment. They amounted to near £20,000, which to pay would have ruined me.

Chapter 8
Final Accounts

As time passed after the great battle, several facts gradually surfaced which not only gave a better perspective to the drama which had surrounded Washington during the battle, they also provided further evidence of the extent to which God had directly intervened in behalf of Washington. For example, one famous Indian warrior who was a leader in the battle was often heard to testify publicly, "Washington was never born to be killed by a bullet! I had seventeen fair fires at him with my rifle, and after all could not bring him to the ground!" When one considers that a rifle aimed by an experienced marksman rarely misses its target, his utterance seems to have been prophetic. It was evident that an invisible hand turned aside the bullets.

A separate verification of the miraculous intervention of God in behalf of Washington is provided through the testimony of Mary Draper Ingels. She was kidnapped from her home in Draper Meadows, Virginia, on July 8, 1755, by a band of Shawnee Indians. Her biography details the amazing account of her capture and subsequent mid-winter escape from the Shawnees after being held captive for several months. Her return trek to civilization covered a grueling 1,000 miles.

At one point, while still a captive at the Indian camp, she recalled a day when the French held a council with the Indians. After the council concluded, the Frenchmen were talking excitedly to each other, gesturing animatedly. Mary listened to their conservation, which focused on George Washington. Having personally met Washington, she began to inquire of the Frenchmen about him. The Frenchmen told her about an Indian chief named Red Hawk who had been in the victory at Duquesne. Red Hawk told of personally shooting eleven different times at Washington without killing him. At that point, because his gun had never missed its mark before, he ceased firing at him, being convinced that the Great Spirit protected Washington. The Frenchmen continued to tell her more details about the battle and its final grizzly outcome. She doubted their account; surely the British could not have been so completely crushed.

After her return to civilization, she related what she had heard about the incident with Washington and the battle for Fort Duquesne. Those in the settlement assured her that what the Frenchmen had told her was indeed accurate.

Fifteen years after the battle, Washington and Dr. Craik, a close friend of Washington from his boyhood to his death, were traveling toward the western territories to explore uninhabited regions. While near the junction of the Great Kanawha and Ohio Rivers, a company of Indians, led by an old, respected chief, approached them. A council fire was kindled and the chief addressed Washington through an interpreter. The chief first explained that after being informed of Washington's approach to that part of the country, he had set out on his long journey to meet Washington personally and to speak to him about the battle fifteen years earlier. Through the interpreter he said:

I am a chief and ruler over my tribes. My influence extends to the waters of the great lakes and to the far blue mountains. I have traveled a long and weary path that I might see the young warrior of the great battle. It was on the day when the white man's blood mixed with the streams of our forest that I first beheld this chief [Washington]. I called to my young men and said, mark yon tall and daring warrior? He is not of the red-coat tribe--he hath an Indian's wisdom, and his warriors fight as we do--himself is alone exposed. Quick, let your aim be certain, and he dies. Our rifles were leveled, rifles which, but for you, knew not how to miss--'twas all in vain, a power mightier far than we, shielded you. Seeing you were under the special guardianship of the Great Spirit, we immediately ceased to fire at you. I am old and soon shall be gathered to the great council fire of my fathers in the land of shades, but ere I go, there is something bids me speak in the voice of prophecy. Listen! The Great Spirit protects that man [pointing at

Washington], and guides his destinies--he will become the chief of nations, and a people yet unborn will hail him as the founder of a mighty empire. I am come to pay homage to the man who is the particular favorite of Heaven, and who can never die in battle.

Eighty years after the battle, a gold seal of Washington, containing his initials, was found on the battlefield. It had been shot off him by a bullet. That relic is now in possession of one of the family. True to the Indian's voice of prophecy, Washington never was wounded in any battle.

So remarkable was his escape from the numerous perils to which he was exposed during the battle that special mention was made in a sermon preached shortly after the battle by the Rev. Samuel Davies, who later became the president of Princeton University. After commending the military qualities which the Virginia provincials had displayed during the fight, Davies added, "I may point out to the public that heroic youth, Colonel Washington, whom I cannot but hope Providence has hitherto preserved in so signal a manner for some important service to his country." How accurately his wish was fulfilled is evidenced by Washington's life.

If the advice Washington offered Braddock before the battle had been followed, and if the Indians had been used as scouts before the advancing army, the ambush undoubtedly would have been discovered and it is very likely that the victory would have been secured for the British. But due to the foolish and haughty arrogance of Braddock, the British were thrown back in a bloody and disgraceful defeat. This, however, resulted in no disgrace to Washington. His fearlessness, perception, and quick decisions in the heat of the battle were praised in the strongest terms by his fellow officers and soldiers. Because of God's help and Divine intervention, Washington gathered acclaim and honor from the same field where his commander received only dishonor and death.

Map of the Battle Area

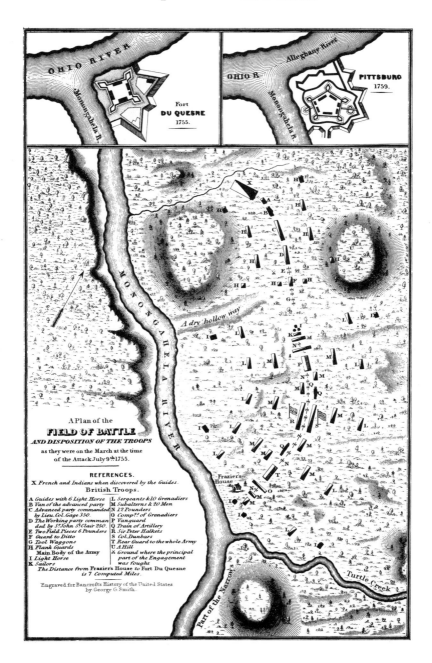

Time Line of Events

1749-1753	Numerous boundary disputes occur between British and French traders
1753	Britain directs Colonies to seek friendship with the Six Nations Indians and also to form a union among the Colonies
31 Oct. 1753	George Washington departs for the French Commander General St. Pierre with a letter from Governor Dinwiddie
12 Dec. 1753	Washington arrives at the French camp
16 Jan. 1754	Washington returns to Williamsburg from St. Pierre
Spring 1754	France reinforces troops in Canada
2 April 1754	Washington takes troops and leaves Alexandria for Will's Creek in first step of repulsing the French
1 May 1754	Washington marches to the Great Meadows
24 May 1754	Washington reaches Great Meadows and constructs Fort Necessity
27 May 1754	Washington captures a French detachment near Fort Necessity
14 June 1754	Council convenes at Albany to construct a union between the Colonies
3 July 1754	Battle at Fort Necessity; Washington attacked by French forces under De Villiers
4 July 1754	Council plan approved by commissioners and then sent to the Colonies and Great Britain for approval
	Washington withdraws from Fort Necessity

20 Feb. 1755   General Edward Braddock arrives in Hampton Roads, Virginia

14 Apr. 1755   Braddock meets with governors in Alexandria; four point campaign against the French is planned

April 1755   General Braddock meets George Washington

20 April 1755   Braddock leaves Alexandria for Will's Creek

10 May 1755   Braddock constructs Fort Cumberland at Will's Creek

30 May 1755   Braddock leaves Fort Cumberland for Fort Duquesne

19 June 1755   Braddock, at Washington's suggestion, divides the army and begins to press forward, leaving Dunbar and the heavy baggage behind

9 July 1755   The Battle at the Monongahela

12 July 1755   Dunbar destroys remaining artillery and baggage

15 July 1755   General Braddock dies

17 July 1755   Washington and troops return to Fort Cumberland

18 July 1755   Washington writes members of his family to inform them personally of the battle

Aug. 1755   Dunbar enters into winter quarters with the British troops

1770   George Washington and Dr. Craik return to the same vicinity as the battle and are met by an Indian chief

Bibliography
Primary Sources

Abbot, John S. C. *George Washington*. New York: Dodd, Mead and Company, © 1875, 1903, 1917, pp. 90-99.

Bancroft, George. *History of the United States, Vol. IV*, 10 Volumes, Boston: Little, Brown and Company, © 1858, pp. 186-192.

Banvard, Joseph. *Tragic Scenes in the History of Maryland and the Old French War*. Boston: Gould and Lincoln, © 1856, pp. 142-159.

Barker, Eugene C.; Webb, Walter P.; and Dodd, William. *The Growth of A Nation*. Evanston, Ill.: Row, Peterson, and Company, © 1928, 1934, pp. 126-128.

Bellary, Francis Rufus. *The Private Life of George Washington*. New York: Thomas Y. Crowell Co., © 1951, pp. 63-116.

Brooks, Elbridge S. *The True Story of George Washington*. Boston: Lothrop, Lee & Shepard Co., © 1895, p. 58.

Franklin, Benjamin. *Works of the Late Doctor Benjamin Franklin Consisting of His Life, Written by Himself, Together with Essays, Humorous, Moral & Literary*, Dublin: P. Wogan, P. Byrne, J. Moore, and W. Jones, © 1793, pp. 122-127.

Goodrich, Samuel G. *Goodrich's Pictoral History of the United States*. Philadelphia: E.H. Butler & Co., © ante 1856, pp. 123-126.

Halsey, Francis W., editor. *Great Epochs in American History, Vol. III: The French War and The Revolution: 1745-1782*, 10 Volumes, New York and London: Funk and Wagnalls Company, © 1912, pp. 39-50.

Harrison, James A. *George Washington: Patriot, Soldier, Statesman*. New York: G.P. Putnam's Sons, © 1906, pp. 65-102.

Headley, J.T. *The Illustrated Life of Washington*. New York: G & F Bill, © 1861, pp. 25-99.

Irving, Washington. *The Life of George Washington*. New York: Thomas Y. Crowell & Co., © 1855, pp. 42-141.

Johnson, William F. *George Washington the Christian*. Milford, Mich.: Mott Media, © 1919, pp. 39-42.

Johonot, James. *The Stories of Our Country*. New York: American Book Comapny, © 1887, pp. 85-94.

Ketchum, Richard M. *The World of George Washington*. New York: American Heritage Publishing Co., © 1974, pp. 30-57.

Lemisch, L. Jesse, editor. *Benjamin Franklin; The Autobiography and Other Writings*. New York: New American Library, © 1961, pp. 140-155.

Lossing, Benson J. *Field Book of the Revolution, Vol. II*. New York: Harper & Brothers, Publishers, © 1852, pp. 471-481.

Lossing, Benson J. *Mount Vernon and Its Associations*. New York: W. A. Townsend & Company, © 1859, pp. 41-43.

Ridpath, John Clark. *Popular History of the United States of America*. Cincinnati, Philadelphia, Chicago, Memphis, Atlanta: Jones Brothers & Co., © 1876, pp. 247-261.

Riviore, Mario. *The Life and Times of Washington.* Philadelphia: Curtis Publishing Co., © 1967, pp. 11-15.

Schull, W.E., editor. *The Story of Our Country by Numerous Writers.* Philadelphia: World Bible House, © 1896, p. 138.

Steele, Joel Dorman; Steele, Esther Baker. *A Brief History of the United States.* New York, Cincinnati, Chicago: American Book Company, © 1871, 1879, 1880, and 1885 by A.S. Barnes & Co. © 1889 and 1900 by American Book Company, p. 84.

Thom, James Alexander. *Follow the River.* New York: Ballentine Books, © 1981, pp. 120-121, 369.

Thwaites, Reuben Gold, and Kendall, Calvin Noyes. *A History of the United States for Grammar Schools.* Boston: Houghton Mifflin Co., ©1912, p. 127.

Weaver, G.S. *The Lives and Graves of Our Presidents.* Chicago: The National Book Concer, © 1897, pp. 48-54.

Willard, Emma. *Abridged History of the United States.* New York: A. S. Barnes & Burr, © 1859, pp. 158-161.

Willard, Emma. *History of the United States.* Philadelphia: A. S. Barnes, & Co., © 1844, pp. 124-131.

Secondary Sources (quoted in the primary sources)

Bradley, A. G. *Fight with France for North America,* "The Defeat of Braddock (1755)," London, Constable & Co.

Custis, George Washington Parke. *Recollections and Private Memoirs of Washington,* Benson J. Lossing, editor, 1860.

Harland, Marion. *The Story of Mary Washington,* © 1892, p. 91.

The Journal of General Braddock's Expedition, in British Museum, King's Lib. vol 212.

Marshall. *Life of Washington,* account by Craik, ii. 19.

Pritt, J. *Mirror of Older Time Border Life,* personal narrative of Colonel James Smith, p. 385.

Report of the Court of Inquiry into the Behavior of the Troops at Monongahela.

Sparks, Jared. *The Writings of George Washington,* 12 Vols., 1834-7, Vol. II, p. 89, p. 474.

Weems, M. L. *The Life of George Washington.* Philadelphia: Joseph Allen, Lippincott, Grambo & Co., pp. 47-48.

Various personal letters:

Washington to his mother 18 July, 1755.
Washington to his brother, 18 July, 1755.
Robert Orme to Gov. Morris, 18 July, 1755.
Vaudreuil to the Minister, 24 July, 1755.
Gage to Albemarle, 24 July, 1755, in Keppel's Keppel, i. 213.
H. Sharpe to Secretary Calvert, 11 August, 1755.
Sir John Sinclair to Sir Thomas Robinson, 3 Sept, 1755.

Sources of Illustrations

Front Cover. Provided by the Union League of Philadelphia Art Collection.

p. 9. "Lead plate buried by the French," provided from the collections of the Virginia Historical Society.

p. 11. "Portrait of Governor Dinwiddie," provided by the National Portrait Gallery in London.

p. 12. "The First Mission of Washington," provided by the Union League of Philadelphia Art Collection.

p. 13. "Washington's Journal, 1754," provided courtesy of the John Carter Brown Library at Brown University.

p. 15. "Death of Jumonville," taken from *The Illustrated Life of Washington,* by J. T. Headley (New York: G. & F. Bill, 1861), p. 47.

p. 16. "Washington's document of surrender at Ft. Necessity," provided courtesy of the Royal Ontario Musuem, Toronto, Canada.

p. 17. "Benjamin Franklin," taken from *A History of the United States For Grammar Schools* by Reuben Gold Thwaites and Calvin Noyes Kendall (Boston: Houghton Mifflin Co., 1912), p. 126.

p. 18. "Join, or Die," by Ben Franklin, provided courtesy of the Historical Society of Pennsylvania.

p. 20. "Braddock," taken from *The True Story of George Washington,* by Elbridge S. Brooks (Boston: Lothrop, Lee & Shepard, Co., 1895), p. 58.

p. 23. "Braddock's Headquarters in Virginia," taken from *The True Story of George Washington,* by Elbridge S. Brooks (Boston: Lothrop, Lee & Shepard, Co., 1895), p. 59.

p. 25. "Advertisement," by Benjamin Franklin on behalf of Braddock, provided by Yale University Library from the "Benjamin Franklin Papers."

p. 27. "On The March," taken from *The True Story of George Washington,* by Elbridge S. Brooks (Boston: Lothrop, Lee & Shepard, Co., 1895), p. 60.

p. 29. "Franklin," taken from *Goodrich's Pictorial History of the United States,* by Samuel G. Goodrich (Philadelphia: E. H. Butler & Co, ante 1856), p. 124.

p. 31. "Plan of the distribution of the advanced party consisting of 400 Men," provided courtesy of the Historical Society of Pennsylvania.

p. 34. "Scene of Braddock's Defeat, 1755," taken from *A Popular History of the United States of America,* by John Clark Ridpath (Cincinnati: Jones Brothers & Co., 1876), p. 260.

p. 35. "The Ambush," taken from *Tragic Scenes in the History of Maryland,* by Joseph Banvard (Boston: Gould & Lincoln, 1856), Frontispiece.

p. 39. "Defeat of Braddock," taken from *The Illustrated Life of Washington,* by J. T. Headley (New York: G. & F. Bill, 1861), p. 60.

p. 41. "Burial of Braddock," taken from *The Illustrated Life of Washington,* by J. T. Headley (New York: G. & F. Bill, 1861), p. 75.

p. 43. "The Indian Allies of the French Return Home...," taken from *The True Story of George Washington,* by Elbridge S. Brooks (Boston: Lothrop, Lee & Shepard, Co., 1895), p. 61.

p. 53. "Map of the Battle Area," taken from *History of the United States,* by George Bancroft (Boston: Little, Brown, & Co., 1858), Vol. IV, p. 188.

Notes

Price List

Prices subject to change without notice.
Quantity & case-lot discounts available.

Books

Original Intent (B16) $12.95
Reveals how the Supreme Court has reinterpreted the Constitution, diluting the Biblical principles upon which it was based.
Relying on primary sources, *Original Intent* allows the Founders
to speak for themselves, describing their intent for America.

America: To Pray or Not To Pray? (B01) $6.95
A statistical look at what has happened when religious principles
were separated from public affairs by the Supreme Court in 1962.

Lives of the Signers of the Declaration of Independence (B14) $9.95
This reprint of an 1848 original provides a glimpse into the lives of
the fifty-six men who signed the Declaration. Learn about these
venerated Americans who helped create this great nation.

Impeachment! Restraining an Overactive Judiciary (B17) $6.95
The American judicial branch is out of control, dominating both
the executive and legislative branches. This book reveals how the
Founders restrained overactive courts via impeachment. Learn
how we can do the same.

Lessons From Nature for Youth (B13) $4.95
First printed in 1836, this reprint will teach young people many
admirable traits once taught in American schools. Learn loyalty
from a buffalo, gratitude from a lion, etc. Great for all ages!

The Bulletproof George Washington (B05) $5.95
An account of God's miraculous protection of Washington in the
French and Indian War and of Washington's open gratitude for
God's Divine intervention.

The New England Primer (B06) $6.95
A reprint of the 1777 textbook used by the Founding Fathers. It
was the first textbook printed in America (1690) and was used
for 200 years to teach reading and Bible lessons in school.

Noah Webster's "Advice to the Young" (B10) $5.95
Founder Noah Webster stated that this work "will be useful in
enlightening the minds of youth in religious and moral principles."

Bible Study Course – New Testament   (B09) $4.95
A reprint of the 1946 New Testament survey text used by the
Dallas Public High Schools.

Bible Study Course – Old Testament   (B12) $4.95
A reprint of the 1954 Old Testament survey text used by the
Dallas Public High Schools.

Guide to the School Prayer & Religious Liberty Debate (B15) $3.95
Explains the issues and answers behind the fight for a Constitu-
tional amendment to protect religious liberties.

"Great Americans" Poster Series *(see product codes & prices below)*
A series of posters designed to give an enjoyable overview of great
men and women in America's history. These beautiful 16 x 20
informational posters are excellent for use in schools.

Poster Set (5 posters) .... (PO1) $19.95
George Washington Carver .... (PO2) $4.95
Thomas Jefferson .... (PO3) $4.95
Abraham Lincoln .... (PO4) $4.95
Pocahontas .... (PO5) $4.95
George Washington .... (PO6) $4.95

Videos

America's Godly Heritage (60 min.)   (V01) $19.95
Explaines the Founding Fathers' beliefs concerning the role of
Christian principles in the public affairs of the nation.

Keys to Good Government (59 min.)   (V05) $19.95
Presents beliefs of the Founders concerning the proper role of
Biblical thinking in education, government, and public affairs.

Education and the Founding Fathers (60 min.)   (V02) $19.95
A look at the Bible-based educational system which produced
America's great heroes.

Spirit of the American Revolution (53 min.)   (V04) $19.95
A look at the motivation that caused the Founders to pledge
their "lives, fortunes, and sacred honor" to establish our nation.

Foundations of American Government (25 min.)   (V03) $9.95
Surveys the historical statements and records surrounding the
drafting of the First Amendment, showing the Founders' intent.

Video Transcripts

America's Godly Heritage (See video)	(TSC01) $3.95
Keys to Good Government (See video)	(TSC04) $3.95
Education and the Founding Fathers (See video)	(TSC02) $3.95
Spirit of the American Revolution (See video)	(TSC05) $3.95
Foundations of American Government (See video)	(TSC03) $2.95

Audio Cassette Tapes

Religion & Morality, Indispensable Supports   (A14) $4.95

Documents the Founding Fathers' belief that religion and morality are indispensable supports for American society.

Thinking Biblically, Speaking Secularly   (A13) $4.95

Provides guidelines for Biblically thinking individuals to effectively communicate truths in today's often anti-Biblical environment.

The Founding Fathers   (A11) $4.95

Highlights accomplishments and notable quotes of Founding Fathers which show their strong belief in Christian principles.

The Laws of the Heavens   (A03) $4.95

An explanation of the eight words in the Declaration of Independence on which the nation was birthed.

America: Lessons from Nehemiah   (A05) $4.95

A look at the Scriptural parallels between the rebuilding of Jerusalem in the book of Nehemiah and that of America today.

8 Principles for Reformation   (A10) $4.95

Eight Biblical guidelines for restoring Christian principles to society and public affairs.

Is America a Christian Nation?   (A16) $4.95

An examination of the writings of the Framers of the Constitution and of the Supreme Court's own records.

The Importance of Duty   (A17) $4.95

Highlights how stewardship of rights and performance of responsibilities is the duty of each Christian.

The Practical Benefits of Christianity   (A18) $4.95

Demonstrates the positive and powerful societal influences which the Founding Fathers believed Christianity provided.

The Changing First Amendment   (A19) $4.95

Shows how court decisions have reinterpreted the First Amendment resulting in rulings opposed to the Founders' intent.

America's Godly Heritage—Part One (See video)   (A01) $4.95
America's Godly Heritage—Part Two   (A15) $4.95
An expanded look at the Founding Fathers' beliefs concerning
the role of Christian principles in the public affairs of the nation.

Keys to Good Government (See video)   (A09) $4.95
Education and the Founding Fathers (See video)   (A08) $4.95
The Spirit of the American Revolution (See video)   (A02) $4.95
Foundations of American Government (See video)   (A12) $4.95
America: To Pray or Not To Pray? (See book)   (A07) $4.95

Pamphlets

The Truth About Jefferson & the First Amendment   (PAM01) $.50
Explains a common misconception concerning Jefferson's role with
the First Amendment and points out those who did influence it.

The Bible in Schools (25 count)   (PAM04) $3.95
A reprint of an essay by Founding Father Benjamin Rush on why
the Bible should be taught in schools.

Order Form

Quan.	Code	Title	Unit Price	Total

When shipping to multiple addresses, cal-
culate shipping based on dollar amount to
each address, not on order total. Thank you.

Sub Total
Tax (TX only, add 7.75%)
Shipping (see chart)
TOTAL

Shipping & Handling

Under $	5.00	$3.00
$ 5.01-$	15.00	$3.95
$15.01-$	25.00	$4.95
$25.01-$	40.00	$6.95
$40.01-$	60.00	$7.95
$60.01-$	140.00	$10.45
Over	$140.00	8%

Please allow 4-6 weeks for delivery.
WallBuilder, P.O. Box 397, Aledo, TX 76008
(817) 441-6044

Bookstores, churches, and organizations (or individuals using Mastercard or
Visa) may call 1-800-8-REBUILD to place an order.